Reading Between The Lions

Gillian Swordy

Illustrated by Leighton Noyes

READING BETWEEN THE LIONS
TAMARIND BOOKS 978 1 848 53004 1

Published in Great Britain by Tamarind Books,
a division of Random House Children's Books
A Random House Group Company

This edition published 2009

1 3 5 7 9 10 8 6 4 2

Set in Pelham infant

TAMARIND BOOKS
61–63 Uxbridge Road, London, W5 5SA

www.tamarindbooks.co.uk
www.kidsatrandomhouse.co.uk
www.rbooks.co.uk

Addresses for companies within The Random House Group Limited can be found at: www.randomhouse.co.uk/offices.htm
THE RANDOM HOUSE GROUP Limited Reg. No. 954009

A CIP catalogue record for this book is available from the British Library.

Printed and bound in China

Bullying goes on in most schools and it's important that everyone works together to root it out.

If you are being bullied, tell a friend, tell a teacher and tell your parents. It won't stop unless you do.

In this story, Lionel is just one of the children being bullied. But because he has support, he faces up to the bully. He soon discovers that bullies are often scared and weak themselves.

Try to find ways of feeling stronger and more confident. If you come across as strong, bullies are less likely to target you.

Find the lion inside you!

Contact **help@bullying.co.uk** *for more help*

OTHER TAMARIND READERS

Ferris Fleet, the Wheelchair Wizard
By Annie Dalton
Illustrated by Carl Pearce

Mum has to go on an important mission for the Cosmic Peace Police. She needs to find a baby-sitter for Oscar, 8, and baby Ruby. They choose Ferris Fleet, the coolest, funkiest young magician ever seen, and his magical wheelchair, Wonderwheels.

An exciting futuristic adventure story!

The Day Ravi Smiled
By Gillian Lobel
Illustrated by Kim Harley

Joy rides at Penniwells Riding Centre and loves it. But she can't quite make Ravi out. She doesn't know he is autistic. She just sees that he's very shy, acts strangely and never smiles. The day he finally does is Joy's best day ever at Penniwells.

This story provides encouragement and inclusion, as well as being a great yarn!

Hurricane
By Verna Allette Wilkins
Illustrated by Tim Cleary

Troy and Nita are sent home early from school because of a hurricane warning. They stop to visit a friend and get caught up in the terrible storm.

Great for discussing weather and its devastating effects.

For my brother, Scot,

who planted the ‘idea seed’

G.S.

For the staff and children of

Sherwin Knight Junior School,

Rochester

L.N.

I’m going to tell a tale today

Which might be useful in its way.

It’s not too long and not too short,

In fact it’s quite my favourite sort.

You might have heard it I suppose,

But this is how the story goes...

When I was young I knew a lad
Whose garden really, truly had
Two lion statues made of stone,
Not baby ones but fully grown!

Now this may come as a surprise,
But if we think of garden size
In nearly every single case
There's not a lot of extra space.

So mostly people do not care
To put enormous statues there.
But this young lad was possibly
The luckiest in history…

For who could ever feel alone
Between two lions made of stone?

But Lionel (the lucky one)
Was actually quite put upon
And like most kids of eight years old
Was not too skilled at being bold,
Especially when singled out

By Picky Pete, the local lout!

"I know my teacher does his best
to save me from this horrid pest.
But Picky Pete is not a fool
And now he gets me *after* school!

I cannot get to school and back
Without the worry of attack…
He says he wants me pulverized
until I'm only peanut-sized!

"And all because I've beaten him
At spellings... (He's a little dim)

It's not my fault he's slightly thick,
He truly is a lunatic!"

It's not uncommon in a school
To find a child who thinks it's cool
To pick on other children there,
To pinch them or to pull their hair,

And Picky Pete was one of those.
He also used to pick his nose...

Then wipe it on his trouser seat
(That's why they called him Picky Pete).

"I don't know what to do at all!"
Thought Lionel...

"That boy is HUGE and partly mad,
I'm stuck with this demented lad!

"I'd give up sweets for half a year,
If only Pete would disappear!
There must be something I can do…
I need some help… I wish I knew
A special, clever, secret way
To make this bully go away."

As usual, when he had enough
Of all the bullying and stuff,
He took a sandwich and a book
And hid where Pete would never look…

Between the lions made of stone
Where past experience had shown
That talking to the lions might
Begin to help him see the light.

To read between the lions was
His favourite thing to do because
He always felt quite safe in there,
And feeling safe was getting rare.

He called them:
Lions 1
and 2

And often asked them what to do.

The one called Lion 2 was nice
And often gave him good advice.
He seemed quite sensible and wise
And never, ever told him lies.

But Lion 1, while still his friend,
Was clearly halfway round the bend.
He often said the strangest things
Like, “Piglets have three sets of wings”
And, “Bumblebees are from the moon.
I’m going there this afternoon!”

Then Lion 2 would heave a sigh
And say, “That’s such a massive lie.
It is not **CLOSE** to being true.
He does not have the faintest clue.”

And Lionel would laugh and say,
"It's fine...
I knew that anyway.

But now you both
must concentrate

(Or think quite hard
at any rate).

I need a plan...
a strategy,
Or Picky Pete will
pummel me.

I'm at the mercy
of this loon,
I need to think of
something soon."

“Well,” Lion 1 cried,

I will make his fingers disappear!
I will chew them up and spit them out.
Oh! Let me bite the little sprout!”

"JUST STOP!"

said Lion 2.

"Desist.

That isn't even

on the list.

It is not wise

to get so wild.

You are not to bite

a single child."

"OH, PLEEEEASE,"

begged Lion 1.

"This once,

Just let me taste

the little dunce.

“Just let me growl and roar and stuff,
That boy is not so big and tough.”

“Then… I’m sure I saw him wink
(He’s not as crazy as we think).”

But Lion 2
said, "What you do
Is find the lion that's in **YOU**.
You don't need courage every day,
It's there inside… but hides away.
So now (and here's the tricky part)

JUST FIND THE LION IN YOUR HEART."

Well, Lionel looked him in the eye,
He cried, "I promise… I will TRY!
For otherwise, I am afraid
I will get mashed to marmalade!"

Sure enough… within the week
He heard the words, "You little freak,
I'm going to pound you into jam,
'Cos that's the kind of boy I am."

But Picky Pete was shocked to find
That Lionel was not inclined
To turn around and run away
The way he would have yesterday.

Instead he stopped and stood his ground
And somewhere from within he found
The courage Lion 2 had said
Was hiding deep inside his head.

He thought, "This is the risky part.
There IS a lion in my heart,
I AM a fierce, ferocious beast…
Bad tempered at the very least.
I can be **DANGEROUS** and **WILD!**"

Then from deep inside this child
(The one with secret teeth and claws!)
There came the mightiest of

A roar that
simply would
not quit.

In fact, I wonder how it fit
Inside this boy who (I have been told)
Was only eight-point-five years old.

"Good grief!" thought Pete.
"He's short, this lad,
but also maybe slightly mad...

This boy has more than one loose screw.
This boy could mince me into stew.
For even though he is quite small
He seems to have no fear at all...

"On second thoughts, I do believe
It might be best if I just leave…"

ARRGGH!

And oh what bliss, what utter joy
To find that Pete is just a boy…
Pretending to be big and tough
Until somebody calls his bluff.
"It's all an act. This boy's a fake.
Well doesn't that just take the cake!

"I half admire the villain's style.
He had me fooled for quite a while.
But Lion 2 was right you see,
The courage WAS inside of me,
So now, when bullies misbehave,
All I have to be is... **BRAVE**.

"But, crikey… that stupendous roar
Has made my throat a little sore.
It's time to have a cup of tea
And celebrate my victory."

I bet you are thinking, "What a cheek,
What piffle... Statues do not speak!
You made it up. It is not true,
A statue cannot talk to you."

And I would say… it IS quite rare,
Those lions were a special pair.
But since that day (you may have heard)
They have not said one single word!

OTHER TAMARIND TITLES

NON FICTION:
The Life of Stephen Lawrence
The History of the Steel Band

BLACK STARS:
David Grant
Rudolph Walker
Benjamin Zephaniah
Lord Taylor of Warwick
Dr Samantha Tross
Malorie Blackman
Jim Brathwaite
Baroness Patricia Scotland of Asthal
Chinwe Roy